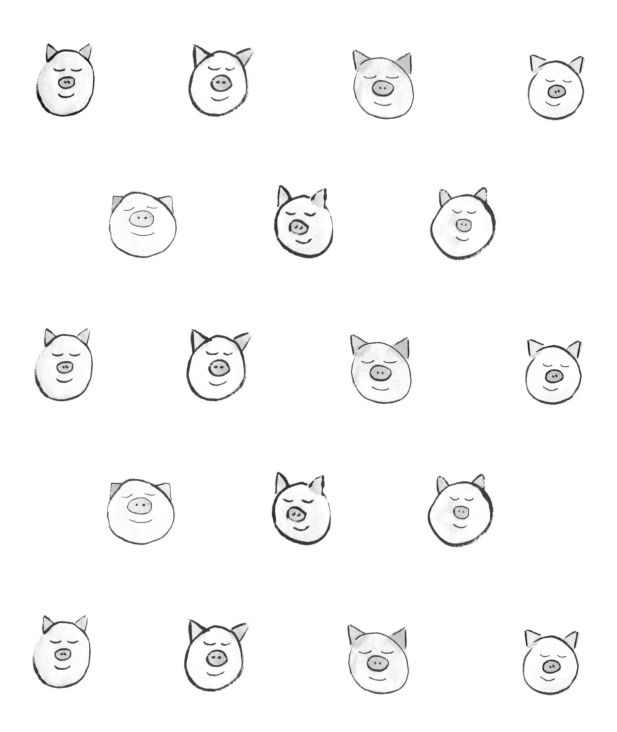

Zen Pig

Book 5

Here To Do

written by:

mark brown

illustrated by:

anastasia khmelevska

Spread the love with...
#ZenPig

Dedicated to LG...

who got back up, chose a better future,
and will soon delight the world.

It was career day again in Zen Pig's town,
Held at the local school.
Zen Pig volunteered to help,
To make sure that it ran smooth.

Shiny badges on police,
Sharp scissors to cut hair,
Fire trucks in the parking lot,
All jobs were presented there.

As Zen Pig helped,
He felt a small tug at his waist.
Smiling gently, he looked down
To find a confused little face.

"Zen Pig, all these jobs look really great,
But I feel like there is something missing.
Does it all just come down to getting a job
And earning a simple living?"

Curiosity piqued overhearing this,
Around Zen Pig, everyone gathered.
Zen Pig took a mindful breath,
Then joyfully gave his answer.

"First, let me say," Zen Pig began,
"That I love how smart you are.
You're asking questions and thinking bigger
There's no doubt you will go far.

These jobs are all important,
That much is true.
But the job is just the vehicle
You pour yourself into.

Choose your career wisely,
But focus even more on who you are.
Remember you are a light,
Meant to shine like a star.

Learn to trust yourself and your purpose.

You are here to look within and listen.

Remember, any thought that sells yourself shor

Is not true – simply put, just fiction.

Avoid overthinking and worrying,
They can easily become an addiction.
Never let a person or even a thought
Stop you on your mission.

You are here to take action,
Make mistakes, and learn lessons.
To get back up, you first must fall,
No one great came from perfection.

The good can only come
From your own caring hands.
Don't look to others to save yourself or the world
We all need YOU to take a stand.

You are a being so expansive,

So unimaginably good,

Your only real job is allowing

Your love for yourself and others to be understood

Namaste.

("The light in me loves the light in you.")

Name: _____

Age: _____ Date: _____

Zen Pig's Question:

What can YOU do to help the world?

_____

_____

_____

_____

_____

Claim your FREE Gift!

 Visit:
PDICBooks.com/Gift

Thank you for purchasing

Zen Pig: Here To Do

and welcome to the Puppy Dogs & Ice Cream family.

We're certain you're going to love the little gift

we've prepared for you at the website above.

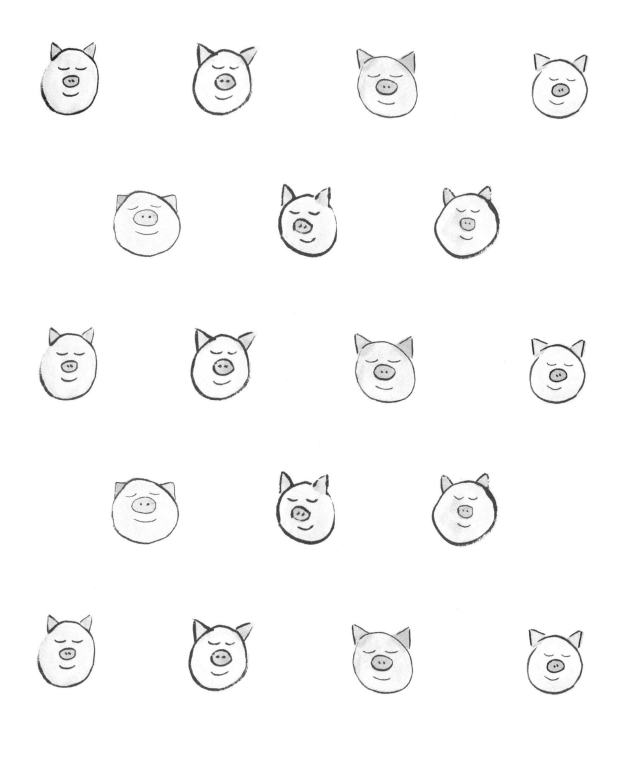

CPSIA information can be obtained
at www.ICGtesting.com
Printed in the USA
LVHW070103240322
714271LV00008B/175

APR 0 5 2022

Date Due
